He's a Hottie!

It's all here! Learn about your favorite Hanson brother, Jordan Taylor Hanson!

★ What's Tay's outlook on life?
★ Where does he get the inspiration for his lyrics?
★ What does he do with his friends?
★ Could YOU be the perfect girl for him?

Find all these answers and more in . . .

Taylor Hanson: Totally Taylor!

Look for Other Biographies from Archway Paperbacks

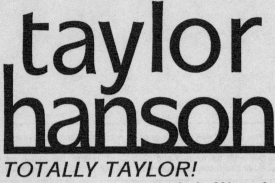

taylor hanson

TOTALLY TAYLOR!
an unauthorized biography

nancy krulik

AN ARCHWAY PAPERBACK
Published by POCKET BOOKS
New York London Toronto Sydney Tokyo Singapore

AN ARCHWAY PAPERBACK *Original*

An Archway Paperback published by
POCKET BOOKS, a division of Simon & Schuster Inc.
1230 Avenue of the Americas, New York, NY 10020

ISBN: 0-671-02371-3

First Archway Paperback printing January 1998

10 9 8 7 6 5 4 3 2 1

AN ARCHWAY PAPERBACK and colophon are
registered trademarks of Simon & Schuster Inc.

Front cover photo by P. Adress/APRF/Shooting Star

Printed in the U.S.A.

IL 5+

Many thanks to Pat Brigandi and Dana Karl

—NEK

CONTENTS

Contents

TOTALLY TAYLOR!

TOTALLY TAYLOR!

Who's your favorite Hanson?

Hanson fans get asked that one a lot. And most of the time, the fans will give an oh-so p.c. (that's politically correct) response. They'll simply say that they love all the guys in the hot new sibling singing sensation. But press those fans to choose just one favorite Hanson, and many of them will have to admit that of the three brothers, lead singer Taylor Hanson is the hottest Hanson!

Taylor, with his big, sky blue eyes, straight, sun-streaked blond hair (that's always parted in the middle), and sweet, shy, pearl-white smile, may be the real reason Hanson changed their name from The Hansons. Rumor has it that some female fans took one look at Taylor and decided that the band should be called The Handsomes.

Taylor, in his usual shy style, won't confirm those rumors. But he won't deny them either. All he will say is, "We used to be called the Hanson Brothers, and then The Hansons, but Hanson is much cooler."

That's true, Tay. Nothing's cooler than Hanson!

On the surface, you might not pick Taylor Hanson to be the most popular member of this *mmm mmm good* group of musicians. Taylor doesn't have his older brother Isaac's deep, brooding, teenage appeal, and he's not the outgoing life of the party, like his younger brother Zac is. And as for rugged sex appeal, that's not Taylor's area either. Some grown-ups have even suggested that Taylor's delicate features have an almost feminine look. (Just another example of how little grown-ups know about hot-looking guys!) But while that might really anger some less secure guys, Taylor characteristically laughs it off. Besides, it was Tay who teased Zac on British radio by telling him that he'd make a really cute girl! (Sorry, Taylor, just like you, Zac's one hot guy!)

Taylor isn't necessarily the kind of guy that seeks out attention. He's more likely to let Isaac speak for the group, or to watch while Zac cracks up a studio audience. In fact, during an interview on *MTV News,* Taylor described himself as the quietest of the three brothers.

But let's face it, lots of girls go for shy guys—

it's a real challenge to think that you'll be the one-in-a-million girl that will wipe away the mask of shyness and be rewarded with a big, welcoming, romantic smile. And what fan wouldn't want to be on the receiving end of Taylor's sweet gap-toothed smile! (Better enjoy that gap while you can, girls. Taylor's parents have informed him that he may soon need braces, just like his big brother, Isaac!)

The true testament to Taylor's overwhelming popularity isn't found on the "We love Tay" signs that fans bring to concerts. If you want to know just how much Taylor's fans love him, hook onto the Internet. You'll find tons of Websites dedicated to Taylor, and Taylor alone. (For more info on Taylor Websites, take a look at chapter seventeen). Visitors to the Websites trade all kinds of private information about Taylor, even down to the color of his toothbrush (one fan swears it's aqua!). But, as Taylor tells his fans, "you'd be surprised what you don't know about me." (Maybe so, but we'd love to find out what we're missing, Tay!)

Taylor's techno fans are amazingly loyal. One fan got so angry at some anti-Hanson propaganda that appeared on the Internet that she posed as Tay and wrote a letter asking the people writing against Hanson to stop. The letter beseeched the anti-Hansonites to stop making fun of Zac because he was just a little kid, and asking them that if they had to dis anyone, to dis Tay.

That, of course, is just the kind of thing a protective and sensitive big brother like Taylor would say. And that's what made the letter so believable. But of course, Tay *wasn't* the author of the computer note. And when it was finally revealed that Taylor himself had not written the letter, the fans didn't know who to be madder at—the kids who'd been criticizing Hanson on the Net, or the girl who'd posed as Tay!

That letter's not the only lie that's gotten passed along on the Web. One report had Tay cutting his hair short! There's no truth to that one. (Tay's already been there, done that!)

Another, more serious, rumor had Taylor being operated on for nodes on his throat. Nodes are tumors that can grow on the vocal chords. The report said that Tay's voice may have been ruined forever by the surgery. Thank goodness that report was completely and utterly false! The only change in Tay's voice has been completely natural and healthy. His voice changed just when most boys' do, around age thirteen. Of course this caused a little bit of concern (and rapid rewriting of musical arrangements) because Tay's big voice change came during the recording of *Middle of Nowhere*. "If you listen closely, you'll hear my voice is about four notes lower at the end of the album than it was at the beginning," Tay admits.

FYI: Tay is a major computer wiz. He has two

laptops! And he does surf the Net. So it's possible that he may just read your note sometime. But, much as he'd like to, Tay can't answer everyone. During a chat on AOL, one fan asked if Tay answered e-mails with a standard letter. But Tay explained that even *that* wasn't physically possible.

"We'd love to respond to as many as we can," Tay insisted in his response. "But look at it now. There are 13,000 online!"

If Taylor is the quietest Hanson brother off-stage, onstage he can be a performing dynamo (just take him away from his keyboards, give him a conga drum, and watch what happens!). Still, Taylor's not likely to be the one to drag a fan onstage—that's more Zac's department.

"We used to give T-shirts away to fans who asked for them. One girl was too shy. She just kind of raised her hand. So [Zac] reached down and pulled her up onstage," Taylor explains incredulously—and with more than just a little discomfort. Taylor has often admitted that Zac's wild antics often embarrass him.

Unlike Zac, when Taylor is confronted with the screams of female fans, he's likely to blush and shout out, "You guys are crazy!" to the adoring throngs. But don't get him wrong. Taylor is flattered by the attention. "It's amazing," he says of the screaming girls. "It's an awesome opportunity for us."

Taylor's position as lead singer in the band gets him a lot of attention—girls always seem to love the singer! Some fans say that all it takes is one listen to a ballad like "Madeline," and you're under Taylor's spell forever. Luckily, Tay's brothers aren't jealous of his place in the spotlight. "There's not a hint of jealousy between any of us. It's not like that at all," Tay told one reporter.

In fact, despite the fact that Taylor sings lead vocals on all but three of the songs on *Middle of Nowhere* (Zac sings lead on "Lucy" and "Man from Milwaukee," and Ike takes on the singing duties on "A Minute Without You"), Taylor doesn't think there *is* a lead singer in Hanson.

"A lot of groups have one singer," Taylor explains. "But the thing that makes us Hanson is that there's three guys who can all sing."

And that's true. It's Hanson's harmonies and sweet blending voices that make them stand out in a crowd. But ask any fan, and she'll tell you that it's *Taylor's* voice that is most identified with the Hanson sound.

Taylor's singing voice comes naturally to him. He's been singing all of his life. "I think it was just a natural progression," Taylor says of writing and performing songs with his brothers. "Our parents would go out and ask us to do the dishes, and they'd come back and we wouldn't have done the dishes, but we'd have written a song. We didn't think about it. It just happened."

Music has *definitely* been a big part of Taylor's life. And even though he's only fourteen years old, you'd be amazed at the exciting life Taylor Hanson led even before his band hit the big time.

BEFORE THE CROWDS

Jordan Taylor Hanson was born on March 14, 1983, in West Tulsa, Oklahoma. He was welcomed into the Hanson family by his mom, Diana, his father, Walker, and his big brother, Clarke Isaac, who was born in 1980. Like his older brother, who was called Isaac or Ike, Jordan Taylor was immediately known by his middle name, Taylor (although his best friends and his fans tend to call him Tay).

Taylor's parents had lived in Tulsa all their lives. So had their parents and their grandparents. Taylor's mother was a music major in college, and his father was an accomplished guitarist. They sang together in a church group called The Horizons that performed around the country. But neither parent ever really thought of making music their profession. And they certainly never dreamed that their children would one day be traveling the globe, singing songs they wrote themselves!

But Diana and Walker planted the seeds of music early in their children's lives. They sang to Ike and Taylor when they were babies. They mostly sang lullabies, but they also composed songs just for their boys. The kids wanted to hear about things that were important in their lives.

"We wrote a lot of songs about frogs and ants," Walker laughs.

Walker and Diana continued singing with the family when Zachary Walker Hanson, better known as Zac, was born in 1985. By then, the two older boys were able to sing to Zac as well.

Taylor has really fond memories of those family sing-alongs. His mom is a big fan of Billy Joel, and as Taylor recalls, "One of the first songs [my brothers and I] sang together was Billy Joel's "The Longest Time.'"

Some of the brothers' earliest harmonies came around the dinner table. Their father taught them how to harmonize when they said "Amen." It started out just being Tay and Ike on harmonies. But before long baby Zac joined in loud and clear.

But music wasn't Taylor's dad's only interest. Like many Oklahoma residents, Walker Hanson was interested in Oklahoma's black gold—oil. He took a job with Helmerich and Payne, an oil drilling and gas exploration company. Walker rose quickly through the ranks, and by 1989 he was the manager of the company's international administration. That's when Taylor's typical Tulsa suburban life changed drastically.

Walker was asked to work in South America for a few months. Both he and Diana thought it would be a great experience for the whole family, so they packed up and spent the next year living in Ecuador, Venezuela, and Trinidad.

Despite the huge lizards, sharp-toothed crocodiles, bats, and rats of the Venezuelan jungle, Taylor recalls his time in South America as being a lot of fun. He could swim every day and experience other cultures most kids can only dream about.

Taylor's schoolwork wasn't interrupted by the trip, either. His mother had already decided that her children would be home-schooled. That means that instead of going to school each day, the Hanson boys set aside a certain number of hours to study with their mom—who was their teacher for every subject including gym!

Diana has dedicated a lot of her life to being her children's teacher. To this day, she's the primary tutor for the Hanson boys while they are on tour.

One of Taylor's most important discoveries

during his time in South America was actually imported from his parents' home in Tulsa. One of the first things Walker and Diana did when they reached Venezuela was set up a tape player. They knew that since music was such a huge part of the family's life in Tulsa, their temporary residence in Venezuela would never feel like home if there weren't tunes playing in the background. Walker and Diana hoped that playing music from home would help curb any homesickness the Hanson boys might feel.

While there were radio stations in Venezuela, the boys couldn't understand the lyrics of the songs played on those stations. Walker and Diana solved that problem by bringing along some tapes they'd gotten from a Time/Life rock and roll compilation series. Taylor and his brothers spent a lot of time listening to hits by Otis Redding, Chuck Berry, Little Richard, and Aretha Franklin.

Before long, Taylor and his brothers knew all the words to all the songs on the tapes. Their dad would pull out his guitar at night, and the whole family would join together to sing songs like "Johnny B. Goode" and "Good Golly, Miss Molly." To this day, Taylor will tell anyone who asks that those early rock and roll hits are the music that inspires him the most.

Old rock and roll is great. Old R&B is great, too. But by the time the boys returned to Tulsa in

1990, they were ready to sing something new. No, not the songs that were playing on Tulsa's top-40 radio stations. The Hanson boys had something else in mind. They wanted to sing songs they'd never heard before. Songs they'd written all by themselves!

3

BECOMING A BAND

According to Taylor, there wasn't any special moment when he and his brothers decided to write their own songs. "We were always singing," he explains.

The Hanson brothers were writing music before they could even read music. They started out singing songs they knew. Then they created original harmonies and arrangements for those existing songs. Finally, they wrote songs all their own.

"We didn't even think about it. It just happened," Tay explains. "There's really no way to predict how you are going to write a song. I would say it's usually music first, because the music is what is inspiring you. A lot of times we just jam, and suddenly the song will be there."

Even Taylor has to admit that some of those

early songs weren't all that great—so you'll probably never hear them on CD. In fact, Tay doesn't even remember the songs, because the guys never wrote them down. They just had the lyrics and the tunes in their heads.

Singing a cappella (without musical instruments for accompaniment) was fun for a while. But before long the guys wanted more. They felt the need to play instruments while they sang. The question was, which instrument should each Hanson play?

Taylor had started taking piano lessons when he was about five. Both Ike and Zac took lessons too, but it was Taylor who could really make that keyboard sing. So, when it came time for the brothers to decide which instruments they would play in the band, Taylor grabbed the keyboards. That was fine with Ike, because he felt the guitar would give him the new and different inspiration he'd been looking for. Ike got his first guitar at a pawn shop. Zac took the only instrument that was left—the drums. His first drum kit was borrowed from a neighborhood pal.

The Hanson brothers had been playing instruments together as a band for only one week when they gave their first live performance. That first show certainly didn't feature the cool, polished sound you hear when Hanson performs today.

"Put it this way," Taylor says, "we got the drums and the instruments, and a week later we played live. But that doesn't mean we weren't good when we played live. It just means we got out there and did it."

"Look, when you start out you aren't as good as you are now," Ike adds.

Okay, maybe that first show didn't make rock and roll history. But Taylor and his bros are musical geniuses—and they're dedicated to practicing. So while it might take anyone else years to master an instrument and learn to play it along with others, the Hansons were making beautiful music together in a matter of a few short months.

During their early touring days, Taylor and his brothers played at local parties and festivals all over Tulsa. They sported neatly coiffed page-boys (!) and dressed in matching outfits. They also developed quite a knack for dancing on-stage. Some people compared their early choreography to that of New Edition.

And while they were touring, the brothers kept coming up with songs. While some musicians labor for days, weeks, and even months over the tunes, harmonies, and lyrics of their songs, composing comes more naturally to Hanson.

Consider the way the boys composed "Thinking of You": "The song 'Thinking of You,' the first song on the album, came when we were just jammin' together," Taylor explained to *MTV News*. "The song just started flowing in, and in thirty minutes, it was written. That's a weird example of how it happens. It happens in all different kinds of ways."

Adding instruments to their a cappella music gave the Hanson brothers a whole new sound. And before long, they were ready to put that sound on a CD. Unfortunately, the recording industry wasn't ready for Hanson. Twelve record labels turned Hanson down! (Ouch! Did you hear that? That's the sound of record company executives kicking themselves . . . hard!)

But that didn't discourage Taylor and his brothers. They just went ahead and recorded their own CD. They called their first independent effort *Boomerang*. It was released in 1995. One reviewer described the tunes on *Boomerang* as "full of slick Boyz 2 Men meets Ace of Base style pop." And although Taylor and his brothers had written more than one hundred songs by that time, the CD included a cover version of a hit by one of Taylor's favorite groups: The Jackson Five's "The Love You Save."

Boomerang wasn't a huge hit. In fact it got hardly any air-play at all. Still, the brothers managed to sell some copies of the CD at their performances at coffeehouses and state fairs. Chances are, if you don't already have a copy of *Boomerang,* you won't be getting one anytime soon.

"It's pretty much out of the loop," Taylor says of the group's first album. "But you never know. We might release it later on."

We can only hope so, Tay!

Before long, the brothers had recorded their second independent CD, *MmmBop!* If you heard the original version of the tune "MmmBop" today, you'd definitely pick it out as the same song you've heard on the radio a thousand times. But the version on the independent CD is slower than the one the boys recorded later on.

MmmBop! did the trick. Steve Greenberg, a vice president at Mercury Records, got his hands on the CD and loved it. (Steve obviously has good taste!) But as he told a reporter for the *New York Times,* at first, Steve wasn't completely certain that the CD was really recorded by three kids.

"I was convinced it was a fake," he said. "I thought the vocals were manipulated or they weren't really playing their instruments."

Luckily, Steve was interested enough to want to hear more. So he agreed to fly all the way from his New York City office to Kansas to hear Hanson play at a county fair. Steve was blown away by what he heard. The next thing they knew, Taylor and his brothers were off to Los Angeles to record their first major album for Mercury Records.

MMMAKING MMMUSIC AT MMMERCURY!

Middle of Nowhere was recorded during five months in 1996. Mercury Records was determined that the album not live up to its name and wind up in the middle of nowhere on the *Billboard* charts. So they brought in platinum-selling songwriters like Mark Hudson (who wrote "Living on the Edge" for Aerosmith), Ellen Shipley (who authored Belinda Carlisle's "Heaven Is a Place on Earth"), and Barry Mann and Cynthia Weil (best known for writing "You've Lost That Loving Feeling" for the Righteous Brothers) to co-write nine of the CD's thirteen tracks with the Hanson brothers. And for overall production of the album, Mercury brought in John King and Michael Simpson, better known as the Dust Brothers.

You don't get hotter in the music industry than

the Dust Brothers. They're the ones who produced the Grammy Award–winning *Odelay* for Beck! And the Dust Brothers can pick and choose who they want to work with. They chose Hanson because the guys compose their own music and play their own instruments.

Now for some kids, being young in such a grown-up industry would be very overpowering. But it's not that way for Taylor. Like his brothers, Taylor has no problem telling the pros how he wants a song to sound. Tay's not shy when it comes to his music. And Taylor wasn't overwhelmed by the star power he was confronted with every day at the studio.

"It's pretty wild," he says of working with such big names in the music industry. "But we love it!"

Every day the Hanson brothers would meet with the Dust Brothers to talk about the way they wanted their music to sound. The Dust Brothers gave some suggestions of their own, adding some interesting elements that Tay, Ike, and Zac might not have thought of. In the end, everyone was pleased with the result.

"I think what the Dust Brothers . . . kinda brought back to our sound was a little of the R&B, with the loops and scratches and sampled sounds, and combined it with pop-rock," Tay says.

Once the album was completed, Mercury put a lot of big label muscle behind promoting *Middle of Nowhere.* They hired Tamara Davis (director of videos for Sonic Youth, Amp, and Luscious Jackson) to direct the "MmmBop" video, and arranged for Hanson guest appearances on MTV's *The Jenny McCarthy Show* and *MTV News.*

"Polygram did a brilliant job of priming the pump. They made sure everyone knew about the band and about the song ['MmmBop']," says one record chain executive. "They shipped advances to the chains and radio stations. Maybe some people missed the hype, but it was hard to avoid."

The strategy worked. "MmmBop" became Mercury's first single in seven years to reach number one on the *Billboard* charts in the United States. To date, the *Middle of Nowhere* version of "MmmBop" has hit the number one spot on the charts in Australia, Austria, Argentina, Belgium, Canada, England, Denmark, Finland, Germany, Hungary, Indonesia, Ireland, Sweden, Israel, Japan, the Netherlands, New Zealand, Switzerland, and the United States. One reviewer suggested that a reason for the song's international success was that the tune's catchy chorus means the same in any language.

Press material for the album carried the headline "Hanson: Where Music Is Headed." The headline kind of embarrassed Taylor. "It's just kind of a marketing thing," he insisted on *MTV News.*

But many music critics agreed with Mercury. Hanson was taking music in a new direction—or back into an old direction, depending on your point of view.

Reviewers seemed relieved to hear some happy music for a change. *Beat* magazine said that "The teenage brothers who make up this Tulsa, Oklahoma, trio are stardom bound and seemingly determined to steer music away from grunge and back to an unabashedly tuneful sound reminiscent of the early rock and roll and Motown eras." *Seventeen* magazine called "MmmBop" "the most infectious style ditty since The Jackson Five classic 'ABC.'" *Entertainment Weekly* agreed, saying that *"Middle of Nowhere picks up where The Jackson Five left off."* And *Faces in Pop* magazine gleefully decreed that "Pop music has once again taken over the world . . . and there seems little question that one band above all of the others is responsible for this somewhat unexpected pop music renaissance—and that's those three blond-haired brothers from Tulsa, Oklahoma, known far and wide as Hanson. Ike, Tay, and Zac have set the world on fire with their rich blend of rock, soul, and pop flavoring."

When *Middle of Nowhere* hit the charts, Taylor was completely and totally blown away! In fact, when he was asked by an *MTV News* reporter how he felt about "MmmBop" shooting up to the number six position after just two weeks in release, all Taylor could say was "It's pretty crazy! To hear Casey Kasem announce on TV that you're on his charts, or to look in *Billboard* and see your name is pretty amazing!"

Yep, Tay and his brothers had sure hit the big time. But Taylor didn't realize just how big the big time was. It took a short trip to New York City for Taylor to see just how much his fans loved him.

As Tay always says, "Everything changes."

But even Taylor Hanson couldn't help but be surprised by just how much things were about to change in his own life.

FANS! FANS! FANS!

Middle of Nowhere was released on May 6, 1997. Taylor and his brothers were turned loose into a whirlwind of promotional interviews. It was their first real taste of the press, but the boys answered questions with humor and humility that surprised just about everyone.

When one interviewer asked Taylor what it was like to be home-schooled, he answered, "What's it like *not* to be home-schooled?"

And when a second interviewer asked him whether being in the world's hottest band had changed him, Taylor replied, "I didn't know we were the hottest band. But it shouldn't change you, and it doesn't."

Perhaps the thing that most threw Tay, though, was the surprise reviewers had at the happiness reflected in many of the songs. In Tay's eyes, the reviewers should be more surprised at the melancholy found in songs by grunge groups like Nirvana and Pearl Jam.

"If music is what you do and you love it, why would you be sad?" Taylor asked one music critic.

The boys' first TV appearance was on *The Rosie O'Donnell Show*. Taylor admits to being a little nervous before the show, but Rosie put the boys at ease. She loved them—and declared them "real cutie patooties!" In return, the guys promised her backstage passes to their performances.

Rosie's show was followed by a chance to play "MmmBop" on *Late Show with David Letterman*. That gave Taylor a real kick. Being on *Letterman* is the ultimate in cool. It didn't even matter that David didn't invite the guys over to the desk for a chat after they played. Taylor knew that Letterman almost never does that. And while the guys were performing "MmmBop" for Dave's studio audience, the governor of Oklahoma had declared May 6, 1997, Hanson Day in Oklahoma!

The *Letterman* show was followed by interviews on *Live! with Regis & Kathie Lee, MTV News,* and *The Jenny McCarthy Show*. Based on Taylor's reaction, he was even more excited about meeting Jenny McCarthy than he was about meeting David Letterman.

"Jenny's really cool!" Taylor told a group of

reporters following the show. His quick grin revealed that Taylor Hanson had succumbed to Jenny McCarthy's charms. (Hey, let's face it, Tay's not blind!)

But it wasn't meeting the celebrities that gave Taylor his biggest kick. It was playing for a huge crowd at the Paramus Park Mall in New Jersey. Taylor had never seen anything like it. Hanson wasn't supposed to go on until eight o'clock, but by seven o'clock the mall was filled with crazed Hanson fans. It took the guys forty-five minutes to get through the crowd and onto the stage. And the screaming from the girls took all the brothers by surprise!

But if Tay was stressed out by the size of the crowd, he didn't show it. And that's a good thing. Because Tay firmly believes that "If you get nervous, you don't act like the normal you."

Hanson flew back to Los Angeles for a record-signing at a Sam Goody store, a taping session for ABC (the boys hosted the first night of the network's new '97–'98 season of TGIF programming), and an appearance on *The Tonight Show with Jay Leno.*

The Sam Goody record-signing was even more wild than the show at the Paramus Park Mall. The video for "MmmBop" was being looped on TV screens throughout the store, and huge electronic banners read "We Welcome Hanson." Fans had been lining up since nine o'clock in the morning to hear the guys sing—at one in the afternoon. The fans had a good reason for coming early—only the first 400 would meet the guys and get their *Middle of Nowhere* CDs signed!

Hanson arrived early to do interviews with the press upstairs. They could hear the fans screaming on the floor below them. The girls screamed through all the songs Hanson performed, too. This time Taylor really got into it. He even encouraged the fans to scream as loudly as they could. The girls obliged, naturally. Later, Hanson signed autographs for a lot more than 400 fans. Some of the really lucky ones got their pictures taken with Taylor, Ike, and Zac.

Hanson was a huge hit on *The Tonight Show,* too, both with fans inside *and outside* the studio. The producers of *Access Hollywood* had been following Hanson during their stop in Los Angeles for a segment on their show. The *Access Hollywood* folks noticed a group of Hanson fans waiting outside *The Tonight Show* studio. The girls had tried but couldn't get tickets to see Taylor and his brothers perform on *The Tonight Show.* They had been waiting outside for hours, hoping to get a glimpse of their favorite Hanson. But so far, they hadn't seen the guys. Most of the Hanson fans had already given up and gone home. But these few girls were tough. They were going to hang in there 'til the end.

The girls' perseverance finally paid off. The *Access Hollywood* producers arranged for the Hanson bros to stop outside and take a few pictures with those devoted fans. *Access Hollywood* filmed the whole thing, of course. And they got a great shot of the sign one girl was carrying. It read (you guessed it!) "I Love You Tay!"

Just goes to show you what kind of kids Tay, Ike, and Zac really are! They never forget the fact that it's their fans who put them at the top of the charts.

After *The Tonight Show* performance, the guys headed back to the airport—and New York City—for an even longer publicity tour in the Big Apple. But this time, nothing would take them by surprise. Hanson was ready to take New York by storm!

ROCKIN' THE BIG APPLE (AGAIN!)

The *Today* show gig was early—after all, the *Today* show goes out live at 7 A.M. Eastern Time. To the untrained eye, this seemed like any other early summer morning in New York City—rush hour in the Big Apple. Commuters and tourists pounded the city pavement, hurrying to reach their destinations.

But this was no ordinary New York morning.

Most of the few hundred people lining the area outside the studio were teenage girls—not your usual *Today* show crowd. But then again, *this was not your usual* Today *show broadcast.*

Many of the girls were wearing choker necklaces made of thick leather cord and various charms. Once again, Taylor was a trendsetter—this time not musically, but in the world of fashion. You'll almost never see Tay without one of his chokers! You'll almost never catch one of his fans without one, either.

Some of the girls in the crowd carried signs that read "I like Ike." Others held banners pledging undying love to Zac. But by far, the majority of the signs were created to get Taylor's attention. Taylor didn't get conceited about the number of signs in the crowd that read "I Love You, TAY!" Instead Tay was, as usual, a little embarrassed by all of the attention heaped on him by his female fans. (And of course, that just makes his fans love him more! Tay is *so* cute when he blushes!)

As the three Hanson brothers stepped out onto the *Today* show's makeshift stage, the crowd went wild. Girls screamed, cried, and cheered for their fave.

Taylor banged his tambourine and began singing the opening notes to "MmmBop." The screams got even louder! But the Hanson brothers didn't miss a beat.

Later on that day, Tay admitted that he's always shocked when girls scream for him. But he was quick to add that he loved it!

"All those girls and guys going crazy," Taylor said. "You just have to have fun with it."

Besides, the noise from the adoring crowd sounded louder to the people on the street than it did to the musicians on the stage. By now, the Hansons know how to protect themselves from the volume of their fans' cheers. All three Hanson brothers always wear earplugs during their gigs.

"It's really cool to think people are screaming at you," Taylor says. "But we'd go deaf [if we didn't wear earplugs]."

Still, rest assured that while the earplugs may keep the volume down, some of the shouting can still get through. So keep on screaming your messages—your voice may just be the one that registers with Taylor or one of his brothers.

Later on that week, the brothers literally stopped traffic during their outdoor performance following the *Fox After Breakfast* show. They performed live outside the show's studio on 26th Street and Fifth Avenue. Hundreds of fans came racing to the area for the surprise concert. The fans sang along—word for word—with "MmmBop" and "Thinking of You," as New York cab drivers honked their horns in a desperate attempt to keep traffic moving.

While the boys were in New York, radio station WPLJ FM sponsored a free Hanson concert. The show was supposed to be held at the Red Oak Diner in Fort Lee, N.J.—just over the George Washington Bridge from Manhattan. But at the last minute, the radio station and the police realized that they had underestimated the band's appeal. The Red Oak Diner would be filled to the rafters with Hanson fans—putting both the fans and the band in danger. So, the radio station moved the concert to the Meadowlands Fairgrounds in East Rutherford, N.J., to allow for the thousands of screaming kids who showed up to hear Hanson perform.

Hanson's second New York press trip was scheduled around September's MTV Music Video Awards Show. Hanson was nominated for the Best New Artist award. They also hosted the MTV Awards pre-show, which featured clips of the guys clowning around in Central Park. The guys really let their hair down on that one. Even shy Taylor ran all over the park and goofed around for the cameras. It was obvious to anyone watching the show that Hanson had become real pros at being in front of the camera!

Luckily, the trip to New York wasn't all work and no play for the Hanson brothers. "We really enjoyed being in New York," Taylor assured his Big Apple fans. "We had a two-day tour and we walked up the Statue of Liberty."

Wow! Imagine being at the top of the Statue of Liberty with Taylor Hanson! Tourists visiting Lady Liberty on that day had a more exciting view than New York Harbor!

Hanson loved New York, and New Yorkers loved Hanson! In fact, the New York metro area hadn't seen anything like the Hanson visit in a long time—not since a band of four lads from Liverpool, England, played at the city's Shea Stadium back in 1964. Those guys were in a band called the Beatles!

Being compared to the Beatles isn't new to

Hanson. In fact, plenty of fan magazines have taken to calling the brothers "moptops"—a term that started almost thirty-five years ago as a description of the Beatles' long hairdos.

Tell Taylor Hanson that he and his brothers are as popular today as the Beatles were in the 1960s, and you'll get one of those big, bright smiles that Tay is so famous for. (Being compared to the Beatles is a pretty big compliment, after all.) But you'll also get an argument from Tay.

"They're the *Beatles!*" Taylor is certain to insist, blown away by the comparison to one of his all-time favorite bands. "Compared to them, we're just ladybugs!"

Maybe so Tay, but hundreds of thousands of fans are really *buggin'* for Hanson!

Taylor may not see any comparison between Hanson and the Beatles, but lots of other people do—especially when it comes to fans of the two groups. It's easy to compare the reaction of the Hanson fans to the screams of the Beatles' fans. In fact, screaming fans were such a big part of the Beatles' persona that they were one of the main focuses of the Beatles' first film, *A Hard Day's Night,* which was a comedy about how the Beatles' lives changed once they became celebrities. The movie opened with the Beatles being chased down the streets of London by screaming female fans as the fab four got ready to perform a live TV show performance. That's a scene the guys from Hanson can really relate to. But Taylor is realistic. He knows that this kind of mania can't last forever.

"It can go as fast as it comes," Tay says of fame. "But for now, it's great!"

But while that fame is still around, Hanson is using it responsibly. To prove how much they care about their fans, Hanson agreed to model for an interesting advertisement. Maybe you've seen it. All three guys sport (slightly premature) white mustaches—milk mustaches, that is! Take a good look at the ad, and you'll have some idea how the guys will look when they're old enough to grow real mustaches. (They'll be absolutely gorgeous, of course!)

The ad asks fans if they've Got Mmmilk, and reminds them that teenagers need at least three glasses of milk a day to keep up with the growth of their bones.

Taylor says he's a milk drinker himself. He'd better be. Tay needs all the energy he can get to handle all of the excitement and craziness in his life.

7

AMERICANS CONQUER THE BRITISH (AGAIN!)

When Hanson arrived in London, one thing became crystal clear. The British had been conquered by Americans, again. The first time it was by George Washington, Paul Revere, and the rest of the freedom fighters. This time the victory went to Hanson!

The trip to London in late May (which was followed by stops in France and Germany) was to promote *Middle of Nowhere*. Rumor has it the boys flew over in coach and not first class, just to prove they weren't anyone special!

But once they were in England, Hanson's visit was incredibly special. Naturally they stayed in a great hotel. And they really got a chance to view the city in a way most visitors never will. While most tourists travel around London on a big double-decker tour bus, Hanson saw the sites in their own way—they went around town with photographers, using the city as their backdrop.

The photographers got their first taste of Hanson charm when they tried to use costumers, make-up artists, and hairdressers on the photo shoot. Ike, Tay, and Zac insisted on wearing their own clothes! Of course, Tay and his brothers weren't trying to be difficult, or insisting on having their own way. It's just that the guys in Hanson know what their fans like. And they know that their fans are happy to see the guys being comfortable and acting like themselves.

"If people ask us to wear things or do poses that we don't want to do, we just try to come up with an alternative," Tay explains. "It's like 'No leopard skin shirts today, thank you very much.'"

The visit to Europe was filled with interviews for radio stations. The ones in France and Germany were done primarily through translators. The London ones, of course, were not, which may explain why Zac said he liked London best—they speak the same language Zac does there.

But Tay also chose London as his favorite European stop. He loved the British accents, and has perfected one of his own.

Traveling to Europe was exciting to Hanson, but probably not as exciting as it might have been to other kids their age. After all, unlike most kids, the Hanson brothers had already had the chance to visit other countries—and to live there. In fact, one of the most exciting moments Tay experienced was right here in the U.S.A. And it was as American as apple pie!

On October 18, Hanson headed down to Florida to sing "The Star Spangled Banner" at the first game of the 1997 World Series! That was a great opportunity for Tay and his brothers. And it was completely appropriate. After all, '97 had made musical champs out of Hanson!

8

AT HOME WITH TAY

Has success changed Taylor Hanson? Not really. He still gets embarrassed when girls whisper about him while he's waiting in line at McDonald's. He's still got to do his schoolwork, and he's not big on the Hollywood party scene. "Usually the three of us [Ike, Zac, and Tay] make our own parties at home, just having fun," he says.

And those parties can be crazy. One time the three brothers invited some of their hometown pals to a party over at their house. They all had Nerf guns and were shooting the guests with foam balls as they entered the house!

No matter what they were doing at the party, it's just nice to know that the Hanson guys continue to hang out with their close childhood friends. And those friends are glad to know the Hanson brothers haven't "gone Hollywood" on them.

Certainly success hasn't changed Taylor enough to make him clean up his room. The room in the Hanson's Tulsa home that Tay still shares with his brothers Ike and Zac is pretty much the way it always has been. "It's a wreck!" he admits.

Of course, Taylor is also quick to tell you that it's not totally his fault. First of all, he does share the room with Ike and Zac. And second of all, the boys haven't been around much to clean it. "We haven't been home in months," Tay explains.

Taylor doesn't keep it much of a secret that he gets homesick when he's on the road. And although Taylor admits that he's spent so much time in L.A. that the family's rented California digs do feel like a home away from home, it doesn't mean he doesn't consider the Tulsa house his real home.

"By the time we finished the [Middle of Nowhere] album, we were ready to come home to Tulsa," Taylor assures his Oklahoma fans.

The Hanson family hasn't bought some huge mansion in Tulsa, either. When the boys come home, they return to the house they grew up in, and the room they've always shared. Sharing a room with his bros is cool with Tay, though.

"We're always hanging out," he says. "We're basically best friends."

"Getting sick of each other is not an issue," Ike adds. "We're brothers and we enjoy each other's company. We like to tease and fight all the time, but it's all in fun."

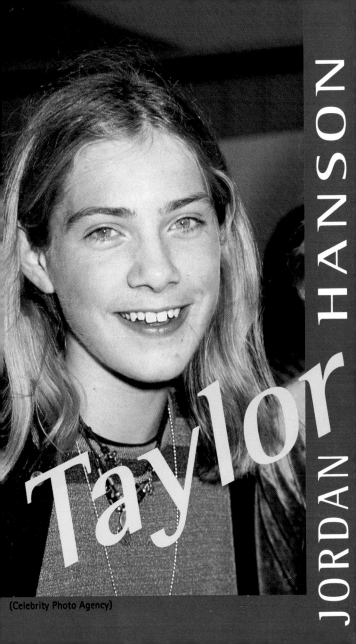

Taylor

JORDAN HANSON

(Ernie Paniccioli/Retna)

(Celebrity Photo Agency)

HANSON

Reaching out to their fans!

Totally Tempting Tay!

If you look around the guys' room, you'll find hundreds of little Lego building blocks—toys that Tay and his brothers have been collecting for more than ten years. These days Taylor's really into the medieval Castle Legos.

Aside from the Legos, there's not much in Taylor's room. The walls don't even have posters on them. Zac likes to joke that none of the guys put posters on the walls—unless they're of themselves of course.

But that's not true at all. What you will find, however, is memorabilia from their tours, like banners, programs, and even a few gifts from devoted fans. There are also two plain white dressers filled with clothes, a broken CD player, and another CD player that works.

The bedroom has only one bunk bed. Ike gets the top bunk, and Taylor gets the bottom bunk. Zac's trundle bed pulls out from underneath.

And then, of course, there's the closet. But Taylor warns all visitors not to go near there. There's something really scary inside the closet.

What could it be? A monster? A bogeyman? A gremlin?

Nope.

"We throw all of our dirty socks in there," Tay reveals.

THE MIDDLE HANSON

Okay, we know what you're thinking. Tay isn't really a middle child. After all, he has only one older sib (Isaac), and there are four Hansons younger than Tay (Zac, Jessica, Avery, and Mackenzie).

All right. So technically Taylor isn't a middle child. But Hanson fans often refer to Tay as the middle Hanson. And the characteristics of middle children often show up in any kid who's not the first born or the baby of the family. So, not so surprisingly, Taylor does fit the description of a typical mid-kid.

Middle children are often more able to go with the flow than their older or younger siblings. But push them to the limit, and middle children will always stand up for what is right.

That's definitely Taylor's M.O. Sure, he's the

quiet one, and the shy one. But say something that he considers wrong, and watch timid Taylor turn into a mountain lion! And when it comes to helping others, Tay's the first one to jump in and lend a hand. He was the first of the three Hansons to agree to play a charity show for the Arthur Ashe Foundation—a group that helps kids with AIDS.

Middle children can often feel left out—they figure there's nothing special about them. After all, they're not the baby, and they're not the first-born. The fact that Tay knows he's special, and can recognize his own talents, is a real tribute to the way Diana and Walker have raised their kids. For one thing, they never compare their children to one another. They encourage each child to find his or her own special talent. And as soon as a Hanson child has found something he or she loves to do, they're encouraged to run with it.

But Diana and Walker don't push. "Our parents have been really good about supporting us in general," Ike told a reporter from the Reuters news syndicate. "They say 'Guys, if you want to quit, quit. But if you want to push harder, let's push harder.' They're always there to back us up."

Tay is not just a fantastic musician with a love for the keyboard, he's a budding artist and cartoonist as well. In fact, he once dreamed of being an animator. To make sure that Taylor knew that his artwork was important to them,

Diana and Walker created a whole art studio in their garage in Tulsa. It's a place where Taylor can paint to his heart's content.

Taylor's artwork may soon be released to the world. A source at Mercury Records says that a future Hanson video may be animated, and that some of the cartoons will be drawn by Taylor. We'll just to have to wait and see!

Taylor is very aware of his parents' support, and it shows in his music. "The alternative thing is fading," he says of the Seattle and grunge musical movements. "People just don't hate their parents as much anymore."

10

TAYLOR TIDBITS

Did you know:
- Hanson is the second-largest act ever to come from Tulsa? (Garth Brooks is the biggest moneymaker to come from the Hanson's hometown.)
- Taylor has a secret passion for country music?
- Taylor's favorite color is red?
- Taylor loves to read and play soccer in what little spare time he has?
- Tay still can't get used to having girls scream at him?
- Taylor's favorite foods are fish and his mom's homemade brownies?
- Tay has three scars: two on his face from running into a glass door, and one on the back of his leg from a soccer game?

- Taylor once broke his arm? As he explains it: "I was going down this huge hill on my bike to see a house my parents thought they might buy. They were driving up the hill as I was coming down, and I saw the car heading toward me. I braked, and went straight over the handlebars. I looked at my arm and it had just snapped!"
- Taylor's hair used to be six inches longer than it is now?
- Tay is ambidextrous?
- Taylor's favorite movies are *Star Wars* and *The Nutty Professor?*
- Tay has a braided rat tail?
- Taylor can be shy—and also flirtatious?
- When he was little he loved running around with a fake sword?
- When he was little he refused to ever, *ever,* take off his baseball cap?
- Tay wears a retainer?
- Taylor takes voice lessons?
- Taylor has a major crush on Jennifer Aniston?
- Tay has a cat named MaMa?
- Taylor's favorite ice-cream flavor is strawberry?
- Tay's favorite soft drinks are mineral water, Sprite, and root beer?
- Taylor's favorite candy is jellybeans?
- Taylor's favorite subject is English?
- Taylor wears size thirteen shoes?

- Tay's favorite soccer player is Alexai Lalas?
- Taylor's favorite Spice Girl is Baby Spice (Emma)?
- Taylor has a habit of tapping out rhythms while he talks?
- Tay shops at the GAP?
- Taylor often wears CKbe cologne?
- Taylor likes to go-cart?
- Taylor wears a lot of blue shirts to make his eyes stand out?
- Ike and Tay really did crash during the filming of the video for "MmmBop"?
- The car that Taylor drives in the "MmmBop" video is the same car Sandra Bullock drove in *Speed 2*?
- When Ike was 11, Tay was eight, and Zac was just six, the guys sang at their father's company Christmas party? It was their first public performance.
- Tay's words to live by are "everything changes"?

11

ARE YOU "TAYLOR" MADE?

Would you believe that Taylor Hanson has put off having a steady girlfriend to make his *fans* happy?! Talk about dedication—and appreciation—to the people who love your music!

"Fans don't like it [when you have a girlfriend]. It's pretty weird. You have a fan asking for your autograph, and you tell her you have a girlfriend, and it's like 'oh, bummer,'" Tay recently revealed to *16 Magazine*. And he also admitted that "We're not looking for now, nor do we have, any girlfriends. We just don't have the time."

But before you let your heart sink too deeply, you should know that Tay wouldn't turn down the perfect girl if he happened to find her somewhere.

"I like girls," Taylor assures everyone, "but I

haven't seen a girl that I can really just go up to without her going, 'Oh my God! Oh my God!'"

Taylor says he'd date a fan—if she wasn't too obsessed with Hanson. "If somebody's obsessed with you, it would be kind of hard to go out with her," Taylor explains. "You'd take her hand and she'd scream! But if she was nice enough, then yeah, I'd date a fan."

Phew! What a relief.

So, how do you know if you're the right girl for Taylor? Well for starters, it would help if you were a bit of a bookworm. Taylor loves to read, and he'd be sure to enjoy spending a cozy afternoon by a fireplace reading with a special someone. But be ready to hone up on that classic literature. Taylor enjoys reading books that are ripe with interesting plots, fascinating characters, and symbolism. Those are the same kinds of elements he puts into his music. Mark Twain is one of his favorite authors.

You'd also have to be very tolerant of Taylor's busy schedule. One of the reasons Taylor doesn't date is that he doesn't feel it's fair to make a commitment to someone and then see her only about one day a month. And with Hanson hoping to take on a U.S. and Canada tour one day soon, Taylor's schedule is going to get tighter and tighter.

Taylor is fond of girls who are direct and honest. There's no beating around the bush where Tay's concerned. And he's kind of confused by girls who just sort of stare at him and point.

"I get embarrassed really easily," Taylor explains. "We were at a McDonald's once, and we were waiting to order our food. All of a sudden there was whispering going up and down the line. People were saying 'Hanson . . . Taylor . . .' and things like that. No one said anything to me. They just whispered. And I was standing there. In the end I just got my food and ran out!"

Imagine the amazing opportunity some girl would have had if she'd only gone over to Tay and said hello. But if you do get the chance to talk to Tay, don't try to compare him with bands from the past. *Especially* the Partridge Family. Tay has always been confused by the comparison people make between a make-believe TV family who didn't even sing their own songs (only David Cassidy and Shirley Jones could actually sing) and a trio of real-life brothers who not only sing, but play instruments and write their own music!

A date with Taylor could get very physical—sports-wise, that is—so you'd better get into shape. Taylor's always up for a quick game of one-on-one, or a pickup soccer game at a local park. Or maybe Tay would take you for a go-cart ride. A bike ride on the beach would fulfill Tay's sports-oriented nature *and* his romantic side. Rollerblading is also one of Tay's fave sports—

it's his way of working off some steam after the pressure of being on the road all of the time.

With all of that activity, you and Tay just might be lucky enough to share an ice-cream soda—strawberry, of course! Strawberry is Tay's favorite flavor!

Of course, sometimes Taylor can be in the mood for taking it easy and just going to the movies. But don't expect to be sharing the popcorn at a real tear-jerker or a boy-meets-girl date flick.

"I don't cry at movies. I watch action movies," Tay explains. "You don't cry at Arnold Schwarzenegger."

As for the make-up, leave it home and in your drawer. Tay is a natural kind of guy, and he likes girls who are happy with their natural selves.

But before you can date Tay, you've got to meet him, get his attention, and really get to know him.

One great way to attract Taylor's attention is to give him a gift he knows took a lot of thought. Despite the fortune he and his brothers are sure to be making on sales of *Middle of Nowhere* (not to mention the school folders, posters, baseball caps, videos, T-shirts, and other items Hanson fans are scooping up by the millions!), money doesn't mean that much to Taylor. Flashing around a wad of cash, or buying him some outrageously expensive gift at Tiffany's, isn't going to catch his attention. In fact, it would probably turn him off completely. Tay would be much happier to learn that you put time and effort into the present, rather than discovering you spent all of your allowance on it. Besides, anything you can buy, Tay can buy for himself, can't he?

The key to getting Tay's attention (or any guy's attention for that matter) is to be creative. Sure, anyone can buy Taylor a huge bag of jelly-beans—by now just about everyone knows that's his favorite candy. You can bet he's gotten more than his share of jellybeans by now! No, Tay's attention will surely be captured by something a little more unique.

One girl in particular caught his eye with a very personal and meaningful gift. In fact, he's still searching all over the world for the one fan who mailed Hanson her entire stamp collection!

"One time some girl sent us this book, and it looked like a collection of stamps," Tay told a radio DJ in Australia. "And we're like 'Oh, she gave us a stamp collecting book.' And we opened it up and it was a complete stamp collection! It was like she'd been collecting for years, and then she sent it to us. She didn't even put her name on it. So whoever it is, we love you!"

And that leads us to an important point—if you're going to send Tay a gift, be sure to sign the card!

Taylor is a gifted artist, and he appreciates that

talent in others. Some of the most eye-catching gifts he's received are portraits of himself drawn by his fans.

"I look at them and it's like, 'Wow! I look better here than I do in real life,'" Taylor exclaims.

That, of course, must be impossible. *Nobody* and *nothing* looks better than Tay in real life!

12

YOU'VE GOT TAY'S NUMBER!

We'll bet you think Taylor Hanson is #1! Well, you're wrong. Taylor is actually an 8. It's true! The letters in Taylor's name make him an 8 in numerology. The science of numerology was dreamed up by the people of ancient Babylon. According to numerology, each person's personality falls into one of nine basic types. And you can find out what type your favorite star (which would be Tay, natch!) fits into by counting up the letters in his name.

How did we figure out that Tay was an eight? We wrote out all of the letters in Taylor's full name, and then matched the letters to the chart at right.

1 2 3 4 5 6 7 8 9

A B C D E F G H I
J K L M N O P Q R
S T U V W X Y Z

JORDAN TAYLOR HANSON

1 6 9 4 1 5   2 1 7 3 6 9   8 1 5 1 6 5

Then we added all of the numbers in Taylor's name together, and got a sum of 80.

But we weren't finished yet. We added the 8 and the 0 (in 80) to get the single-digit number 8. That makes Tay an 8 (in numerological terms only, of course! Everyone knows that in looks and talent, the guy's a perfect 10!).

So what does this all say about Taylor? A lot. Eights are incredibly self-disciplined people, with high powers of concentration. They are born leaders (or in this case lead *singers)* who like to work hard for causes. If they aim high, they almost always reach the top! Eights make great friends—but very bad enemies. Don't ever cross an eight—they never forget. Then again, they never forget a kindness, either. Good matches for eights are twos, fours, sixes, sevens, and nines.

What's your number? And what does it say about you? Are you the perfect match for Tay?

Check it out! Here are some of the personality traits for the other numbers.

According to numerology, **ones,** like eights, are natural-born leaders. They are extremely well-organized, and tend to like to do all of the work themselves. Ones love the spotlight! But they can also get a reputation for being selfish and ruthless, so they have to learn to give up the limelight once in a while and share the glory. Ones get along well with twos and sixes.

Twos are more quiet and reserved. They're fair, and are always looking to understand both sides of a situation. Twos are good friends who have amazing memories and love to talk over old times. But twos can also be super sensitive. Criticism makes them brood over hurt feelings. Twos also need to learn to stand up for themselves a bit more often. Twos make good matches for sevens, eights, and other twos.

Threes are dynamic—but rarely domineering. Still, they like having things done their way, and they'll fight to get it. Threes like feeling comfortable in any situation, and they know how to make others feel that way, too. Threes are a lot of fun to be around, but they have sharp tongues that can sting. Everyone thinks they know all there is to know about a three, but nobody really does. Threes get along especially well with fours and fives.

Fours take duty and responsibility very seriously. But they are never dull and boring. Fours can be witty and entertaining, as well as being incredibly loyal pals. But they need to watch the annoying habit they have of saying exactly what's on their minds. Fours get along very well with twos, threes, and eights, but they really go for fives and sixes (which can be a dangerous combination!)

A **five's** restlessness will forever keep her on the go. What a five likes is action, adventure, and plenty of excitement. And fives are always the life of the party. Fives should look at careers in communications. But be careful: Once they get jobs, fives tend to let their salaries slip right through their hands. Fives absolutely cannot hold on to money. They get along well with threes, sevens, and twos.

People who are **sixes** spend a lot of time worrying about other people's welfare. It's hard not to like a six because they are so kind, even-tempered, and eager to help. But sometimes sixes can be a little too trusting. People think of sixes as easy marks, and tend to take advantage of them. Sixes need to develop a little more backbone. If you're a six, spend some time hanging out with ones, eights, and nines.

Sevens are trendsetters! They are always full of new and exciting ideas. They can also be deep thinkers who love to delve into a subject. But a seven never seems to feel that she's done enough research, or that her term paper is complete enough. Nobody sets higher standards for themselves than sevens! Lighten up and enjoy life a little, you sevens out there!

People think sevens are snobby, but they're not. Sevens are just really shy people. Sevens get along really well with nines, fours, sevens, and eights.

If you are an **eight,** take a look at the numerological characteristics we listed for Taylor on page 53. Your personality should be similar to Tay's! Cool!

Nines are true humanitarians. But sometimes that can mean trouble, because the needs of their close friends and family can take a back seat to their concern for humanity's big picture. Nines are likely to use their money and their seemingly endless stamina to help the world. But when it comes to a nine's own feelings, she's extremely mercurial—up one minute and down the next! Fours, sevens, and eights make great matches for nines.

THE STAR'S STARS!

Taylor's birthday is March 14. That makes him a Pisces. And Pisces is certainly the sign that fits Taylor. Pisces are extremely creative people. They're also imaginative, intelligent, and . . . (no surprise here), musical! Sometimes it's really amazing just how close astrological signs can be to a person's true personality.

Pisces people are really easygoing. It takes a lot to anger them. That's why Tay doesn't get mad at people who tease him about looking like a girl, or at his brothers, who like to tease him about his accessories (those ever-present chokers and his wristwatch). But watch out when you criticize something Tay really cares about, like his music, his art, and especially his family! Pisces don't get mad often, but when they do, their tempers can explode. Luckily these few incidents always blow over quickly. And Pisces are quick to forgive.

If the stars are correct, the girl that finally does grab Taylor's heart will be one lucky lady. Romance means a great deal to a Pisces man. Flowers, candy, fireplaces, the whole deal! (Sounds nice, huh?)

But Pisces isn't Taylor's only astrological sign. He's also a real Boar. No, we didn't say bore, we said Boar. According to the Chinese zodiac, anyone born in 1983 was born in the year of the Boar.

The theory behind the Chinese zodiac is that your birth year can influence how you act and even foretell what kind of career you might try in the future. The unique thing about this system is that each birth year is named for a particular animal. The people born under that sign supposedly take on some of the characteristics of that animal, as well as other characteristics. A boar is a wild male pig.

People born in the year of the Boar are extremely dependable, which may explain why during recording sessions it was always Taylor who made sure his brothers kept their minds on their music. And it may also explain why Tay can get annoyed when Zac changes the beat of a tune in the middle of a show. Since the drummer does drive the beat of the song, Tay and Ike have to change their tempos with Zac's beat. Tay always keeps up with his brother's tempo changes (he is dependable and a professional after all), but Tay also likes to be able to depend on others.

People born in the year of the Boar can never just sit around doing nothing. They are always involved in a lot of activities. That explains why Hanson's whirlwind press tours and performance schedules never wear Taylor out. He's actually stimulated by the constant motion and excitement. It also explains why in his spare time, he rarely sits around vegging on the couch and watching TV. With such a small amount of free time, Tay would rather catch up on his reading, drawing, or sports.

Most of the time, Boars are the leaders of any groups they are involved in (say a musical group like Hanson). And Boars always set good examples for others, which fits right in with Taylor's passionate anti-drug and alcohol stance.

In Taylor's case, we guess you could say: Boars never bore! Boars rule!

14

THE ULTIMATE TAYLOR HANSON MUSIC LIBRARY

The way to Taylor's heart is not through his stomach. Everyone knows that Taylor's real love is music. His current faves include Counting Crows, Spin Doctors, and Natalie Merchant. It's a little hard for him to believe that suddenly these big name artists are not only among his favorites, they're among his competitors! Such is the price of fame.

Although Taylor likes all kinds of music—top 40, country, gospel, grunge, rock, and even rap—it's the music he heard as a young child that Taylor likes to listen to most often.

You can hear the influence of these musical greats in every song on *Middle of Nowhere*. Listen for the gospel-tinged rock tune "I Will Come to You," The Jackson Five–esque "Where's the Love," and the Beatles-influenced ballad "Lucy."

Taylor is very proud of the diversity in Hanson's music. He always reminds his fans to "Listen to every song [on *Middle of Nowhere*] because there is a huge variety of songs. One makes you want to dance, one makes you feel good, one is really intense, and another is really mellow." It's kind of like having a whole record collection in one awesome CD!

Do you want to tune in to Taylor's musical faves (and ensure that you'll have something to talk about if you meet him)? Then why not stop by the local record store (or dig through your mom and dad's record collection) and check out some of his favorite recording artists? Who knows, you may just find these artists sneaking onto your stereo—after you've had your daily dose of *Middle of Nowhere,* of course!

CHUCK BERRY

Chuck Berry is one of the enduring legends of rock and roll. Some people think that he's rock's number one influence. And he's certainly influenced many of rock's legends. Chuck Berry's hits of the 1950s caught the ear of two young English boys—John Lennon and Paul McCartney, sparking their interest in rock and roll. Mick Jagger and Keith Richards also list Chuck as one of their early idols. In fact, Elvis Presley, the Beatles, and The Rolling Stones all dug into Chuck's repertoire for some of their early hits.

If you're looking for some familiar songs to rock with, check out these songs: "Roll Over Beethoven," "Johnny B. Goode," "Sweet Little Sixteen," and "Come On."

LITTLE RICHARD

Little Richard wasn't just an influence on Taylor Hanson. He's been a major contributor to the careers of almost everyone in rock and roll. Maybe that's why he's always disputed Elvis Presley's title as the King of Rock and Roll. Little Richard is pretty sure he's the real king.

Why not decide for yourself? Take a listen to his greatest hits—"Tutti Frutti," "Long, Tall Sally," "Rip It Up," and "Good Golly, Miss Molly"—and see if you don't think the title is rightly Little Richard's!

OTIS REDDING

Taylor has always loved Otis Redding's rhythm and blues sound. And Taylor has a special connection to Otis Redding—Otis started his singing career in his church choir, just like Taylor's parents did.

If you're in the mood for some hot rhythm and blues (Taylor says he's *always* in the mood for good R&B!), check out these Otis Redding classics: "Sittin' on the Dock of the Bay," "Pain in My Heart," and "I've Been Loving You Too Long."

ARETHA FRANKLIN

They call her the Queen of Soul, and when Aretha belts out a tune, you know why. Like Otis Redding, Aretha got her start singing gospel music, and that gospel sound has never left her. One of her most famous albums is *Amazing Grace,* which Aretha recorded with her father, a minister at the Bethal Baptist Church in Detroit. If soul is your sustenance, then check out Aretha's version of Carole King's "Natural Woman." Then take a listen to these solid-gold Aretha Franklin hits: "Respect," "Baby I Love You," and "I Say a Little Prayer."

THE BEATLES

John Lennon, Paul McCartney, George Harrison, and Ringo Starr were quite possibly the most famous men of the 1960s. As the Beatles, their music transcended generations—and helped to bridge the generation gap. Like Hanson, the Beatles wrote and recorded songs in many styles—rock, pop, soul, romantic ballads, and even avant-garde. And although they recorded together for just seven years, their songs will probably live on forever.

It's the early Beatles songs that have most influenced Taylor. So pull out your parents' old Beatles LPs (if you still have a record player in your house) and give a listen to classics like "She

Loves You," "I Wanna Hold Your Hand," "Can't Buy Me Love," and "Yesterday."

THE JACKSON FIVE

Before Michael Jackson was known for building private amusement parks and the moonwalk, he was the lead singer in a group made up of Michael and his brothers (sound familiar?). The Jackson Five were part of the Motown music scene—a group of African-American recording artists that included The Four Tops, Marvin Gaye, The Temptations, and Gladys Knight and the Pips. All of the artists at Motown were discovered by recording industry genius Berry Gordy, who during the 1960s created the Tamla Motown organization, which at its height was the largest African-American-owned corporation in America.

If you're in the mood for some family harmonies—and listening to Hanson is sure to get you in that kind of mood—check out these red-hot Jackson Five hits: "I Want You Back," "The Love You Save," "ABC," and "I'll Be There."

THE SUPREMES

The Supremes were another of Motown's hottest acts. Headed up by the amazing pipes of Diana Ross, the all-girl trio took the country by storm in the 1960s with huge number-one hits like "Baby Love" and "You Can't Hurry Love."

BILLY JOEL

You already know that Taylor's mother was a total Billy Joel freak, and that she taught them to sing "The Longest Time" a cappella. But Billy Joel has had a huge string of hits, and like Hanson, he can write and sing songs in a number of styles. Take a listen to the Beatles-esque sounds of "Laura," the epic storytelling lyrics of "Scenes from an Italian Restaurant" and "Piano Man," and hard rockin' tunes like "Uptown Girl" and "You May Be Right."

15

TAY'S FANS SPEAK OUT!

So what do the fans have to say about Tay? Lots! Here's what just a few of Tay's thousands of fans think about the blue-eyed hunk with the world's sweetest smile.

Taylor Hanson is the kind of guy every girl loves. When I look at him my heart melts. His voice is so sweet, it makes me want to hear him again and again. He's got so much talent.

Even though Taylor sings most of the songs, we can't forget about Zac and Isaac, who make Hanson complete. Hanson is the cutest bunch in the world. They will always be *MmmBop*ping in my mind, even when I *get old and lose my hair*.

—Jessica

I think Taylor is a very good singer and it's awesome that he started at such a young age. I would love to hear Hanson in concert and get a chance to meet him, because he seems like a really nice person.

—Dana

I was really lucky. I got to see Hanson at the [Paramus Park] Mall. They were awesome. Tay looked so cute! Everyone was screaming, and singing, so I couldn't really hear him too well. The only embarrassing thing that happened was that my mom started singing along.

—Nicole

I'm totally into Hanson. I especially like Taylor because he's fourteen and so am I. This summer everybody I know was really into Hanson, too. But then they got tired of hearing "MmmBop," and they didn't like Hanson anymore. But I didn't get tired of them at all. I'm really glad they have a new album coming out for Christmas, because now my friends will get back into Hanson music.

—Diana

Taylor is definitely the cutest Hanson. He's got those great eyes, and the best voice of all. And I

love his necklaces. I just bought one with the
same Egyptian symbol (an ankh) that he wears. I
read in a magazine that it's supposed to bring
good luck.

—Julia

16

LOOK INTO THE CRYSTAL BALL

What's coming up for Taylor Hanson? Well, believe it or not, the next few months are going to be even more exciting than the summer and fall of 1997.

First of all, Tay's going to get to do the thing he loves most—perform! And that's gonna be pretty cool, because although the Hansons have been celebs for almost half a year, this will be the first time they're appearing before huge arena crowds. Take their October 30 concert, for instance. They filled up Chicago's Rosemont Horizon Indoor Theater. Then on November 16 they headed down to Miami to take part in the huge Gloria Estefan show.

These shows (and the tour that is sure to follow) promise to be more incredible than anything Hanson has ever done before. It's a lot more elaborate than the sing-alongs they've done in shopping malls and with TV audiences.

Taylor insists he'll be choosing his own clothes for the group's new gigs.

"Originally we thought we'd all match," he says. "Or at least be color-coordinated. But we kind of said this is all too corny. So we decided to just wear what we want to wear and be comfortable." The best fashion news of all is that Tay has no plans to cut his hair!

One album is not enough to fill a whole concert. So Hanson will be adding some of their favorite R&B tunes to the mix. Now's the time to pull out your folks' old albums and learn the words. You're sure to want to sing along when Hanson rolls into your town.

Some lucky fans might actually get to meet Hanson after their shows. The guys plan on signing autographs between the performances at two-show-a-night gigs—unless the crowd size gets too big. If at any time there seems to be a danger to the guys—or to their fans—they'll have to call a stop to the autographs. Hanson is always protected by security, but their fans aren't. And Hanson wants to make sure that no one gets injured in a rush from the crowd.

The concerts are sure to make Tay happy. As Taylor says, "We just want to keep performing. We want to keep going in the business. We also want to produce—music and movies!"

Well, Taylor and his brothers may not be up to producing yet, but they are making new music. Their new album was released on November 18, 1997, just in time for the Thanksgiving and Christmas holidays. The album's name is *Snowed In.* (And who wouldn't want to be snowed in with Tay?!)

Snowed In features original songs by Hanson, as well as some classic R&B. There's even a few rock and roll holiday hits, like Charles Brown's "Merry Christmas Baby." Mark Hudson, the man who co-wrote some of the tunes on *Middle of Nowhere,* is the producer of the guys' new release.

And of course, a new album means new videos. A source at Mercury Records says the guys will be even more involved in making the new videos than they have been with the ones in the past.

"They are thinking of copyrighting cartoon characters they've drawn and putting them in as recurring characters in their videos. But knowing them, they'll want each video to be completely different."

And speaking of videos, one week after the release of *Snowed In,* Tay and his brothers gave their fans another holiday treat—an all new home video called *Tulsa, Tokyo, and the Middle of Nowhere.* The video features live musical clips, as well as footage of the guys in their hometown.

As if a new album and new concerts weren't enough to keep fans drooling with excitement, Tay has a few more surprises in store for his adoring fans. Hanson had their own ABC-TV special in late November, to coincide with the release of *Snowed In*. And that's not the only place you'll be able to use your remote to bring Tay into your living room. Hanson is scheduled to be the musical guest on a December *Saturday Night Live*. Forget your beauty rest that night—stay up late and watch!

As for Tay's personal future, rest assured that there's no truth to the rumor that a solo album from Tay is in the making. There's no way Tay would break up the band. He loves being with his brothers. And he truly believes that it is the group's harmonies—and not Tay's solo voice—that keeps the band as cool as they are. And to make sure Hanson's sound stays sweet, Tay is busy taking voice lessons. He's learning how to take control of those amazing pipes of his now that his voice has changed.

In the next few months, Tay may find himself in a completely new position at concerts—in the audience. It seems the three younger Hanson children—Jessica (age 9), Avery (age 6), and Mackenzie (age 3)—may want to form a group of their own. And big brother Tay is sure to be there, cheering them on and helping in any way he can.

No matter what the future holds for Taylor, Ike, and Zac, Tay insists one thing is certain.

"We'll always be striving for the next best thing," he promises.

And we can't wait to hear what Taylor comes up with!

17

TAY CHAT

There are tons of Websites dedicated to Taylor and his brothers on the World Wide Web. So get ready to interface with other Tay fans. Here are some addresses to Hanson and Taylor Hanson Websites. (Other than the Official Website, not all of these may be available when you try them. Websites tend to come and go, y'know.)

Hansonline (the Official Website)
http://www.hansonline.com/

Links to Other Cool Hanson Sites
http://members.aol.com/Crescent14/hlink.html

Becah's Taylor Hanson Web Page
http://www.geocities.com/RainForest/7320

Hanson Fact Sheet
http://members.aol.com/GSquiggles/
  hansonfacts.html

If you're not on the Net yet, you can still get current hot info on Taylor Hanson (and Ike and Zac as well!). Just send your name and address along with a stamped, self-addressed #10 envelope to: HITZ list, P.O. Box 703136, Tulsa, OK 74170.

18

THE TAYLOR TRIVIA TEST!

So you think you know all there is to know
about Hanson's hottest hunk. Well, maybe you
do. But then again, maybe you don't. Take this
Taylor Trivia Test and find out! You'll find some
of the answers to the questions written within
the pages of this book. But some of the questions can only be answered by the most adoring
Taylor Hanson fans. You can check your answers on pages 80–83.

1. True or False: Taylor and his brothers sang a
   cappella at a Tulsa festival called AprilFest.
2. Who tutors the Hansons when they are on
   the road?
3. What is Taylor's middle name?
4. What is Taylor's favorite song on *Middle of
   Nowhere?*

5. True or False: Isaac once told Taylor to blow his nose on the radio.

6. Who is Lucy?

7. Which three *Middle of Nowhere* songs doesn't Taylor sing lead vocals on?

8. True or False: Taylor is the best Rollerblader of the three Hanson members.

9. Which two songs did Hanson perform on *Regis & Kathie Lee?*
   A. "MmmBop" and "Lucy" B. "Weird" and "Madeline" C. "MmmBop" and "Madeline"

10. What children's toys do Taylor and his brothers collect?
    A. G.I. Joes B. Legos C. Beanie Babies

11. What are Taylor's two favorite sports?
    A. Rollerblading and tennis B. Fly-fishing and skiing C. Soccer and basketball

12. What sign was Taylor born under?

13. What is Taylor's nickname?

14. What is Taylor's favorite hobby?

15. True or False: Tay does one mean Kermit the Frog imitation.

16. What two instruments does Taylor play during Hanson concerts?

17. True or False: Tay came up with the idea for the song "Weird" after seeing a talking cat on a TV show.

18. What is Taylor's favorite fast-food joint?
    A. McDonald's B. Burger King C. Wendy's

19. True or False: The Hanson brothers used

stunt doubles to do their Rollerblading on the video for "MmmBop."

20. True or False: The Hanson family lived in Paris for six months.

21. What famous sign could the Hanson brothers see from the house they rented in California while they recorded *Middle of Nowhere?*

22. What city do the Hansons call their second home?

23. True or False: The name Taylor means one who is a tailor.

24. Which of these two do Hanson not give their adoring fans—autographs or hugs?

25. What record label is *Middle of Nowhere* recorded on?

26. What is the name of Hanson's first independent album?

27. What color are Taylor's eyes?

28. What former teen idol wrote "Where's the Love?" with Taylor, Ike, and Zac?

29. Which grunge star has Taylor been compared to—Eddie Veder or the late Kurt Cobain?

30. What is Taylor's favorite soft drink?

31. True or False: Taylor once dreamed of being a cartoonist.

32. True or False: Tay isn't allowed to date until he's seventeen.

33. Taylor's favorite TV shows are:
A. *The Rosie O'Donnell Show* and *General Hospital* B. *Beavis and Butthead* and *Freak-*

azoid C. *Monday Night Football* and *Space Cadets*

34. True or False: Taylor's parents were once in an a cappella fifties group.
35. Which *Middle of Nowhere* song mentions the words "middle of the road"?
    A. "Where's the Love" B. "Man from Milwaukee" C. "Madeline"
36. What is Taylor's favorite color?
37. True or False: Taylor's hair is really light brown. He dyed it blond just the way Sting did when he was in the group The Police.
38. By what nickname do *Middle of Nowhere*'s producers go by? (Hint: They've also produced albums for Beck and The Beastie Boys.)
39. True or False: Taylor prefers hiking boots to sneakers.
40. How old was Tay when he began taking piano lessons?
41. Who is Taylor's best friend?
42. Which Hanson brother most embarrasses Tay?
43. True or False: Tay, Ike, and Zac wrote or co-wrote all but one song on *Middle of Nowhere*.
44. Name the second of the two independent albums Hanson released prior to *Middle of Nowhere*.
45. True or False: Tay is the only member of Hanson who can play the piano.

46. True or False: Tay once had his beautiful blond mane styled in a pageboy.
47. True or False: Tay got his first keyboard at a pawn shop.
48. What does Hanson call their fans?
49. For whom did Tay, Ike, and Zac write the *Middle of Nowhere* cut "With You in Your Dreams"?
50. True or False: It makes Tay crazy that Zac uses the word "weird" so often.

ANSWERS TO THE TAYLOR TRIVIA TEST

1. False, it was the Mayfest.
2. Their mother, Diana. She's been home-schooling the boys their whole lives.
3. Taylor
4. None of the songs is Taylor's favorite. He loves all of the songs—each one has a special meaning for him.
5. True
6. She's the character from the Peanuts cartoon strip. The song is written from the point of view of the character Schroeder.
7. "Lucy," "Man from Milwaukee," and "Minute Without You."
8. False. In fact, he falls a lot!
9. C
10. B
11. C

12. Pisces
13. Tay
14. Playing arcade games
15. False. It's Isaac who imitates Kermit.
16. Keyboards and congas
17. False. Actually, according to Taylor, "We were talking about the fact that nobody had ever written a song about 'weird.' It seemed strange to us. Think about how many times you say the word 'weird.'"
18. A
19. False
20. False
21. The Hollywood sign
22. Los Angeles
23. True. Maybe that explains why Taylor is Hanson's trendsetting fashion expert. His chokers have set a whole new totally hot fashion craze!
24. The Hanson guys sign their names, but they won't give out hugs—sorry!
25. Mercury
26. *Boomerang*
27. Blue
28. Mark Hudson of the Hudson Brothers
29. Kurt Cobain
30. Bottled water
31. True
32. False. Taylor can date now if he wants to—he just doesn't have the time.
33. B

34. False
35. B
36. Red
37. False
38. The Dust Brothers
39. True
40. 8
41. Ike
42. Zac
43. False. They wrote or co-wrote every song on the album.
44. *MmmBop!*
45. False. All three guys know how to tickle those ivories!
46. True
47. False. That's where Isaac got his first guitar.
48. The Scream Squad
49. Their grandmother who died
50. False. Actually it's Tay who says "weird" all the time.

How Did You Rate?

38–50 correct: Congratulations! You know more about Taylor than his brothers probably do!

25–37 correct: Give yourself a hand. You are a true Taylor fan!

15–22 correct: You know something about Taylor, but not a whole lot. Are you sure you're not really a closet Ike or Zac fan?! (That would be cool—Ike and Zac are phenomenally cute and talented too, y'know!)

10–14 correct: Pull out those fan mags or get on the Net—you have some studying to do. But face it, studying Taylor is a lot cooler than studying for your science quiz!

0–9 correct: Where have you been the past few months—in the middle of nowhere?!

ABOUT THE AUTHOR

Nancy E. Krulik is a freelance writer who has previously written books on pop stars New Kids on the Block, rap stars M.C. Hammer and Vanilla Ice, and teen actors the Lawrence brothers. She's also written for several Nickelodeon television shows. She lives in Manhattan with her husband and two children (who *love* Hanson!).